What Are We Fighting For?

Brian Moses performs his poetry and percussion show in schools, libraries, theatres and festivals around the UK and overseas. Over a million copies of his poetry books and anthologies for Macmillan have been sold. Find out more about him at: **www.brianmoses.co.uk**

Roger Stevens is a children's author and poet who visits schools, libraries and festivals performing and running workshops. Roger also runs the Poetry Zone, a website for children and teachers: **www.poetryzone.co.uk**

Other books by Brian Moses and Roger Stevens

100% Unofficial! Olympic Poems
Brian Moses and Roger Stevens

A Cat Called Elvis
Brilliant poems by Brian Moses

Beware! Low Flying Rabbits
Poems by Roger Stevens

The Truth About Parents
*Hilarious rhymes by Paul Cookson, David Harmer,
Brian Moses and Roger Stevens*

The Truth About Teachers
*Hilarious rhymes by Paul Cookson, David Harmer,
Brian Moses and Roger Stevens*

What Are We Fighting For?

Illustrated by
Nicola L.
Robinson

NEW POEMS
ABOUT
WAR

BRIAN MOSES AND ROGER STEVENS

MACMILLAN CHILDREN'S BOOKS

First published 2014 by Macmillan Children's Books
a division of Macmillan Publishers Limited
20 New Wharf Road, London N1 9RR
Basingstoke and Oxford
Associated companies throughout the world
www.panmacmillan.com

ISBN 978-1-4472-4861-3

To the memory of both my father, Harry Moses, whose 'During the war . . .' stories I often failed to appreciate as a child, and my father-in-law, John Joseph Ford, who, at fifteen years old, ran away from home to join the army.

(BM)

For my father, Tom Stevens, who drove a tank in the Second World War and told me the story of tanks passing by, and my father-in-law, Roy Pryor, who was in the Royal Army Medical Corps and was captured at Dunkirk, and who still tells me what life was like as a prisoner of war.

(RS)

Contents

The Second World War 33

The First
World War

'Swear by the green of the spring that
you'll never forget'

Siegfried Sassoon

The Great War

The First World War
Was known as the Great War
The War to End All Wars
Because it was hard to imagine
A darker war, a deadlier war
A grimmer or a grimier war
A scarier or a nastier war

A better name would have been
The Not-So-Great War
The Miserable War
The Senseless War
Or
The War That Did Not End All Wars
Or
The War That Taught Us Nothing

Roger Stevens

The Angels of Mons

Did the British have divine protection
in the first months of the war,
and was something seen on the battlefield
that had never been seen before?

Was there really an army of angels
when the British thought they were beat?
Were there shining figures among the clouds
that protected the British retreat?

Was the German cavalry stopped in its tracks
as the horses refused to advance?
And was it a supernatural sight
that gave the British a chance?

Some say that it was spectral figures
with flaming swords that lit the night.
Others say bowmen fired arrows
tipped with bright pulsating light.

Whatever happened soldiers escaped
when really they should have died.
And the Angels of Mons showed British troops
that Heaven could be on their side.

Brian Moses

*Some British soldiers claimed to have seen visions in the sky while
retreating after the Battle of Mons, August 1914.*

Smile Please

I saw some old newsreels
Of the Great War

And I saw young men
From the towns and villages of Britain
Smiling for the cameras
Smiles as wide as sunshine
Like they were going on holiday

But as the French winter set in
And the mud in the trenches
Got thicker and colder

And more of their friends died
From bullet wounds
From explosions
From poisonous gas

The young men
Wading up to their waists in freezing mud
Tending the wounded and the dying
Were no longer smiling for the cameras

I saw some old newsreels
Of the Great War
And wondered
What were we fighting for?

Roger Stevens

The General's Message on the Morning of Battle

It's a beautiful day for a battle,
the sun is shining bright,
birds are high in the sky,
it's a lovely day for a fight.

God is on our side, lads,
he's sure to help us win.
We're fighting the good fight,
impatient to begin.

The war will soon be over,
the war will soon be won.
We just need one more push to
help us rout the Hun.

Good luck to every one of you,
play up and play the game,
we've beaten them at football
and again we'll do the same.

So come on lads, do your duty,
it's over the top you go.
I'll be with you there in spirit
as you race to meet the foe.

Our enemy is weakened,
we're sure to have them beat.
But just in case we don't,
I'll be leading the retreat!

Brian Moses

The Hun – First World War slang for German soldiers

Christmas Truce

'Hey, Tommy, you like tobacco?'
'Hey, Fritz, have my bottle of beer.'
'It's Christmas Day,
goodwill to all men, so,
what are we doing here?'

And maybe it would have stopped
then and there, once Tommy and Fritz had realized
that both were ordinary men.
That both had families,
girlfriends, wives,
that both were a long, long way
from anywhere anyone
called home.

And all that sad, strange Christmas Day,
Tommy and Fritz shook hands with each other,
sang together the Christmas songs
that both discovered they knew.
They joked with each other
through gestures and signs,
in a language that needed
no words.

Then a football was found
and they played a match,
two nations in the midst
of war, the score unimportant.

And it finished with a rifle shot
that sent men back to their dugouts.
Shouts of, 'Merry Christmas, Tommy,'
and, 'Happy New Year to you, Fritz.'
'Meet you again tomorrow,
show you photos of my girl.'

But it wouldn't do
for the guns to stay silent
or to think of your enemy
as a friend.

The rules of war
are clearly defined,
and someone must win
in the end.

Brian Moses

Tommy – First World War slang for British soldiers
Fritz – First World War slang for German soldiers

Home by Christmas

Victor watched as his dad
chained his bike to a tree
then waved goodbye
as he went to war.

Home by Christmas,
everyone said.
By then the war will be won,
the danger gone.

'I'll have had an adventure
in a foreign land,
something to tell grandchildren
in years to come,'
his dad had told him.

'We'll be welcomed back like heroes,
dancing in Trafalgar Square,
celebrating with our loved ones.
We'll be safe, alive and well.

'And no, it won't be dangerous,
we won't be there for long.
Just watch the lane,
I'll be riding back,
you'll hardly know
that I've gone.'

And all Victor wanted
was his dad to be home for Christmas lunch,
for the war to be over and won.

But sadly all Victor could see
was an empty place at the table,
a bike still chained to a tree.

Brian Moses

When the First World War began in August 1914, most British families thought it would all be over by Christmas. Unfortunately, the war continued until November 1918.

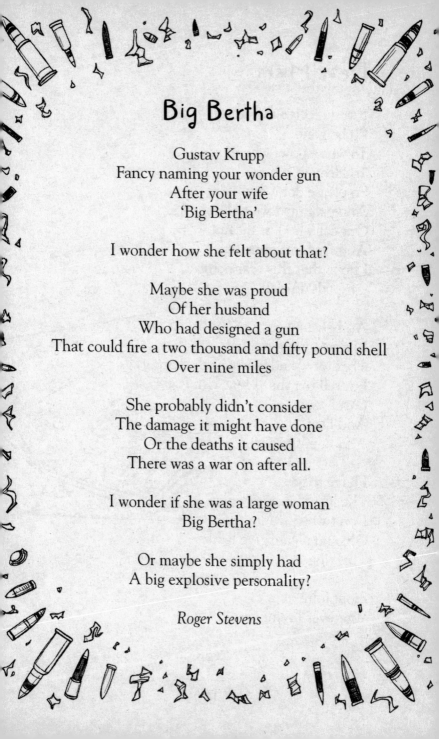

Big Bertha

Gustav Krupp
Fancy naming your wonder gun
After your wife
'Big Bertha'

I wonder how she felt about that?

Maybe she was proud
Of her husband
Who had designed a gun
That could fire a two thousand and fifty pound shell
Over nine miles

She probably didn't consider
The damage it might have done
Or the deaths it caused
There was a war on after all.

I wonder if she was a large woman
Big Bertha?

Or maybe she simply had
A big explosive personality?

Roger Stevens

Dear Mum

If you receive this letter
I'll be gone
To who knows where?
To Heaven, I hope.
So please don't cry.
And give my love to Lop,
Our cat who lost his tail.
And Dad, of course.
I hope that this year's crop
Of spuds do well.

And give my love to Ruth
I know I promised her
That we would marry in the spring
But tell her that I love her
(And you
And Dad
And Lop, the cat).

I have to go
The big offensive's come
Don't worry, Mum
Oh, and please give Ruth
This ring.

From John
Your ever-loving son

Roger Stevens

Goodbye Note

I'm saying goodbye to England,
from a trench somewhere in France.
Saying goodbye to my girl
and our fun at the Saturday dance.

Goodbye family farm,
goodbye house on the hill,
goodbye to the fields,
the river and the gill.

Goodbye to the silence,
the solitude and the peace,
goodbye to home-baked scones
and my mother's family feast.

Goodbye to the hens I tended,
goodbye to my dog and my mouse,
to the cows at rest in the byre,
to the swallows that circle our house.

A fond goodbye to my school,
where I was taught the recourse
to settle any argument
was words, and never force.

Till here with the rattle of gunfire,
the bayonets, the blood,
the wounded and the dying,
the screaming and the mud.

There's little chance that I'll escape
a bullet or a shell,
I'm saying goodbye to all I love
and saying hello to Hell.

Brian Moses

Gill – narrow stream through a wooded ravine
Byre – stable

*Soldiers in the trenches would often keep a letter to
their loved ones on their person before they went into
battle, to be sent home if they died.*

The Colour of
Your Skin

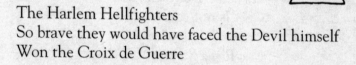

You would have thought
That in a war
The colour of your skin
Would make no difference

But in the Great War
Only white American soldiers
Were allowed
To die in glory

The Harlem Hellfighters
So brave they would have faced the Devil himself
Won the Croix de Guerre

But returned to America to find
Their deeds of heroism
Ignored

Today you might find this story
Hard to believe

Roger Stevens

Croix de Guerre – medal awarded by the French government to soldiers
who fought for France during both world wars. More than 200,000 African-
Americans served in the First World War. The majority of men worked in
labour divisions although about eleven per cent fought in combat forces. They
served in segregated divisions (the 92nd and 93rd) and trained separately.

When Your Name's Not on the List

Every week
The names
Of the dead
And missing
Are pinned up
On the church noticeboard

And Mum
Gives me a lovely safe squeeze
Because Dad's name
Is not there

Roger Stevens

Somme

In the Battle of the Somme
First of July
Nineteen sixteen
Over nineteen thousand soldiers died
And half a million fell

And fighting with the French
Young Canadians, Australians, Bermudians and Indians
Newfoundlanders, New Zealanders
South Africans and British
Joined the Germans in that hell

One hundred years on
In the green and pleasant Somme
You'd hardly know there'd been a war
But for the story that the nineteen thousand poppies
Tell

Roger Stevens

Tipperary

'It's a long way to Tipperary, it's a long way to go . . .'

It was almost *his* song,
'Tipperary'.
His parents' farm five miles from town.
Tipperary, the place
they drove cows to market.

And all it took
was the babble of rooks
in the yew trees of French villages,
the smell of wild garlic
on the breeze at night,
and he was there,
Tipperary.

'It's a long, long way to tickle Mary,'
they sang on marches.

And Mary was the name
for every girl they'd left behind.
But not him.

Sixteen, never been kissed,
enlisted illegally.
Trumpets, fanfare,
bit of a dare really.

Till two years on and war-weary,
eyes closed, sun on his face,
he'd think himself there.

'It's a long long way to Tipperary,'
he'd hum.

Till opening his eyes he'd discover
how far it was
and always would be.

Brian Moses

The Nation at Home

At first, the nation at home hardly knew there
    was a war on.
There were no TVs transmitting the news into
    every sitting room.
No mobile phones sending video footage live
    from the front.
No satellites beaming back images of troop
    movements.
No tweeters on Twitter.
No way you could Google the Somme.
They hardly knew there was a war on,
knew nothing of the terror, bayonets
    charging machine guns.
Till one day the newspapers showed
    soldiers stumbling from trains.
The walking wounded, bloodied
    and dazed,
bringing the war back home.

Brian Moses

Trench Warfare

the sTench of death
in the cRowded trenches
breathing smokE and hot ash, the rattle of
machine guNs, animals struggling to
haul the heavy Cannons through the mud
and the terrified Horses strain, stumble
while we are up to our Waists in freezing water and muck
the whistle blows! Attack! we say a hurried prayer
we scramble oveR the top, across barbed wire
so many Friends fall, retreat
only the deAd can escape this hell
and for yeaRs the living dream of
explosions, I wakE up shaking and scared

Roger Stevens

Abandoned Dog

Abandoned dog
found wandering in no-man's-land.
A Labrador bitch
or something like it,
coal-scuttle black.
Chalky saw it, kept calling.
His family had dogs
before the war, a dozen or so
in a farmhouse
on the North York Moors.
The dog didn't trust him at first
but he offered food
and she must have been starving.
Came back each night,
lucky she wasn't shot.
Then one time she stayed,
played with Chalky.

He knew the right place
to stroke her,
to keep her calm.
You could tell she'd been through hell,
every noise spooked her.
Chalky understood, eased her
beneath his blanket.
'Lucky' he named her.
Lucky for him too,
as a gentle rhythm, heart against heart,
brought both the stillness they needed.

Brian Moses

*During the First World War, some dogs were trained to
take messages from one part of the battlefield to another.
Other dogs were abandoned by their owners and were
stranded in the middle of a battle as the front lines advanced.*

Tanks

Over rough ground
Over trenches
Squashing barbed wire
Walls and ditches
Returning fire
Machine guns deadly
Two six-pounders
Moving slowly
Caterpillar tracked
And weighted
Stuck in craters
Armour-plated
Soldiers inside
Hot and breathless
Fumes and cordite
Easy targets
German bullets
Armour piercing
Tanks advancing
Fiercely crossing
No-man's-land
But by war's ending
The Tank Corps had
But four remaining

Roger Stevens

*The first tank was used in battle in 1916. The word 'tank' was in fact
a code word and was short for 'mobile water tank', so spies would not
realize that the British were actually building mobile armoured weapons.*

Luke and Jessie

Luke was nineteen when he died.
His gravestone gives no information
about where or how and signals just one of a million
    deaths that year.
His fiancée Jessie was sixteen when the news came
    back, along with her photo from his tunic pocket
    where he'd kept her close to his heart.
The love of her life,
she grieved his passing, never quite found
anyone else who triggered the feelings she had
    for her soldier boy.
She visited his grave, laid flowers.
She grew old,
as he never did.
One hundred years when she died, knowing again
    she'd be with him. Together then, together now,
for eternity.

Brian Moses

*Private Luke Leadbetter was killed in 1917. His grave can be seen in the
Aeroplane Cemetery near Ypres. His fiancée Jessie arranged for her ashes to
be laid on his grave when she died eighty-four years later.*

Pals

Harry and Spud, Rawlings and I,
we were pals.
We lived in the same street,
attended the same school.

When war broke out
we joined up.
Seemed right somehow,
the four of us, together,
doing our bit
for King and Country.

It was hard at first,
but there were laughs too.
Harry and Spud, Rawlings and I
helped each other through.

We sang the songs,
not tunefully, but
enthusiastically.
I remember Spud
serenading Harry:
'If you were the only girl
in the world,' he warbled,
till Harry thumped him.

And laughter was the key
to keep our spirits up
when all we had
to look forward to
was mud and blood and bullets.

No idea why I survived
and they didn't.
One of the lucky ones
me, kept my head
below the parapet
and somehow the bullets
passed me by.

I've lived in the same street
all my life, and every year the wife
and I stand here on Remembrance Day
while I say a prayer for Harry and Spud
and Rawlings.

I run my fingers
over the names, etched in stone,
remember where their lives were lost,
and how we won the war,
but at what cost?

Brian Moses

Conscientious Objector

Nineteen sixteen and half a million dead
Volunteers thin on the ground and the
    government said
Now you have to fight

But Danny Jones had read the Bible
Love your enemies, Jesus said
Fighting isn't right

So Danny joined the Red Cross
Stretchered the wounded through the trenches
In the dying light

And what he saw, no man should see
So do not question Danny's bravery
When he refused to fight

Roger Stevens

Bravery

After Adrian Mitchell

Over the top
In the face of enemy fire
Bravery
I like that stuff

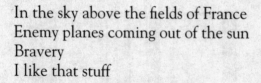

In the sweltering, airless
Sweat-box of a tank
Bravery
I like that stuff

In the sky above the fields of France
Enemy planes coming out of the sun
Bravery
I like that stuff

Defusing a bomb, rescuing
A child from a firebombed house
Bravery
I like that stuff

Fighting, fighting, killing, wounding, maiming
All for a piece of land?
War
I hate that stuff

Roger Stevens

Pip, Squeak and Wilfred

Rummaging in the attic
I found a rusty OXO tin
With three medals in
Grandma said
The bronze Mons Star
Has her dad's name on the back

The British War Medal shines silver
St George, sword raised
Trampling the enemy's skull and bones

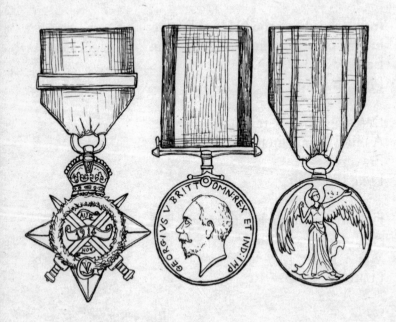

The Victory Medal weighs heavy
And Winged Victory stretches out her arm
A goddess claiming all the world as her own
And on the back
The Great War for Civilisation

Grandma said they were nicknamed
Pip, Squeak and Wilfred
After a cartoon family of orphaned animals
In a *Daily Mirror* cartoon strip

Pip the dog
Squeak the penguin
And Wilfred the long-eared rabbit

Almost everyone won a medal
Grandma said.
If you survived that war
You deserved it

Roger Stevens

Cenotaph

Grandma
Told me about her dad
How he'd comb his hair
Wear his Sunday suit
(Only once a year
He'd wear a tie)
To make that long, slow walk
      to the Cenotaph
On a dark and chilly November
      morning
His medals polished
And pinned to the front
      pocket
To remember all those
      soldiers and friends
Who fell
Who never won a medal
Who never made it to
      December

Roger Stevens

*A cenotaph is a monument used as a
memorial to honour a person or group
of people whose remains are elsewhere.*

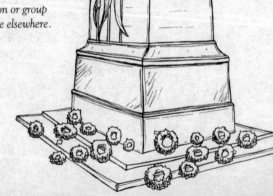

The Second World War

'Never in the field of human conflict
was so much owed by so many to so few'

Winston Churchill on the Battle of Britain

3rd September 1939

It seemed as if
it was just another ordinary Sunday.
Looking back I recall that
Mum and Dad were quieter than usual,
kept exchanging looks that they thought
we didn't notice. The cat was fed
then brushed herself against my legs.
There were eggs for breakfast
as there always were on Sunday.
Mum didn't eat much and we thought
perhaps she wasn't feeling well.
We could tell there was something
the matter. Dad snapped at us,
said to eat, not chatter. So we did,
Billy and me, then kicked at each other
under the table. 'Ow!' Billy yelled.
'That hurt.'
'You'll both have something
to yell about, if you keep that up,'
Dad warned.
'Go on,' he said,
'get out of our sight.'

An hour later we tiptoed back.
The house was quiet except
for the radio's crackle, and then
a sombre voice spoke the words
that nobody wanted to hear:
'This country is at war
with Germany.'

Brian Moses

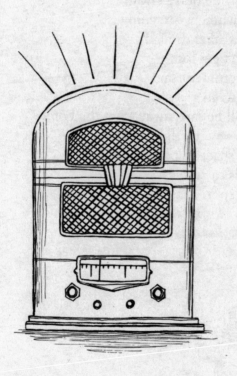

Evacuation

I dunno why Mum's crying so
We'll be fine
Got on the train to Wales
My sister and me
And a hundred other children
Heading for the sunshine
Although we don't know
Exactly where we're going
I've got a label though
So I won't get lost
The government said
We had to go
And we'll be safe, away from the bombs
And anyway it will be exciting
All that space to play in
And hills to climb
And sheep to chase
So I don't know why Mum's crying

Roger Stevens

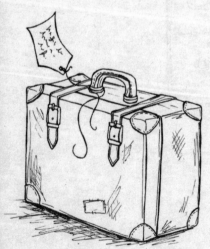

Mollie

It was fine, all the time
she had Mollie,
as much as a rough sea and
a bucking boat could ever be really fine.
Leaving Guernsey, that feeling
of being lonely, but not alone,
with friends, but not family.
She'd always travelled with her parents before
and now she'd left them behind.

So she clutched the doll, held her close,
tried to smile, tried to eat something,
to look on the bright side, as Mum would say,
put a brave face on it.
But somewhere between the ship and the train,
on the rainy streets of Weymouth,
in the hustle and bustle of a hurried chase
to reach the station on time,
Mollie must have fallen from her pocket.

It wasn't till the train hissed and set off
that she realized Mollie was missing.
Her teacher's hugs, her soft voice,
the sympathy of her friends,
nothing could console her, the tears
ran fast and freely.

And in the hours and hours it took
for the train to steam its way north,
the loss of the doll seemed
a link in a chain, now broken.
She and her family driven apart.
They, still in danger on Guernsey,
while she journeyed on to find
a new home with strangers.

Brian Moses

*Parents in the Channel Islands had to choose between
keeping their children with them or sending them to
the British mainland. Many children faced a long sea
crossing followed by an even longer train journey to
the north of England.*

Letter from Two Elderly Ladies Who Volunteered to Do Their Bit and Help the War Effort by Taking in Evacuees

Dear Sir,

We'd like to swap our evacuees,
    we don't like the ones we've got! They're messy and they're smelly, they've got lice and they swear a lot.
    We thought we'd be getting children who knew how to be polite,
    who didn't fight all the time and could tell wrong from right.
    We thought they'd be kind and grateful for the food we give them to eat,
    but they seem to ignore the vegetables and only eat the meat.
    The chickens have stopped laying eggs they're chasing them everywhere.
    The cat just won't come near them since they pulled out tufts of his hair.
    It isn't Christian we know,
    but we just can't take any more. Every day the neighbours
    come knocking on our door.
    So can we swap our evacuees? I'm sure

they don't like us. We're sorry to have to ask,
   it's not like us to make a fuss.

Yours faithfully,

Lizzie & Florence Abercrombie

                              Brian Moses

Another War

It wasn't just a war between the Germans and the Brits
it was a war between the vackies and the village kids.

It was a war of words, a war of stones,
it was a war that threatened broken bones.

It was village kids with faces of granite
as if they belonged to some other planet.

'Go back home, we don't want you here,
go back where you came from, disappear.'

It wasn't just a war between the Germans and the Brits
it was a war between the vackies and the village kids.

It was 'us and them', it was 'them and us',
it was mud fights causing family fuss.

Kids were rolling around in the dirt,
thumping each other and getting hurt.

Bloody noses and cauliflower ears,
the noise of jeering and lusty cheers.

It wasn't just a war between the Germans and the Brits
it was a war between the vackies and the village kids.

It was big 'uns bullying and little 'uns crying,
it was twisted arms and fists that were flying.

It was, 'See you later for a fight after school!'
and, 'Chicken if you don't show, that's the rule.'

'You vackies will regret ever leaving your town
because we're the gang here and we'll knock you
    down.'

And it wasn't just a war between the Germans and the
    Brits
it was a war between the vackies and the village kids,
it was a war between the vackies and the village kids.

Brian Moses

Rude Noises

It winds our teacher up
when we make rude noises
through our gas masks.

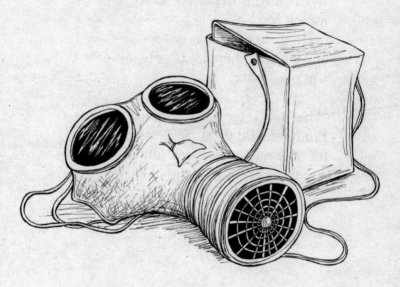

We take it in turns
to breathe out quickly
till the rubber vibrates
and the noise escapes.

Then if we're feeling
that he deserves
some real aggravation,
we start up our
rude-noise orchestra.

We find it amusing,
we find it fun,
but he seems to have lost
his sense of humour.

'We're meant to practise every day,'
we tell him,
putting our gas masks on
and wearing them for twenty minutes
while we work.

'That's all very well,' our teacher says.
But he should think himself lucky,
it's only rude noises after all,
and there is no lingering smell!

Brian Moses

No Surrender

'There will be no surrender.'

It was a statement from Winnie in a stern and
    passionate speech.
It was scrawled in vapour trails on a canvas of sky
    above Kent.
It was the man in the rubble that once was his
    home, shaking his fist at the sky.
It was soldiers defiant on Dunkirk's beaches wading
    out to warships.
It was Auntie Doris pounding a pub piano while
    the sirens sounded.
It was 'There'll Always Be an England', 'Rule,
    Britannia!' and 'Jerusalem'.
It was eyes filling with tears at the sight of the flag.

'There will be no surrender.'

And there wasn't.

Brian Moses

*'Winnie' was the affectionate name for Winston Churchill, Britain's Prime
Minister for most of the Second World War.*

Photograph

Here's the photo I took
Last year on the beach
Dad wearing the tie
I bought him for his birthday
Billy drinking lemonade
The straw up his nose
And Mum huddled up in her coat
Against the seaside wind

Now Dad's in France
And our beach is covered in concrete
And tangled barbed wire
And landmines
In case the Germans invade

But on that day
We'd just made
The world's grandest sandcastle
And watched the tide
Rush in
Filling the moat
Gradually washing
It all away

Roger
Stevens

The Little Ships

Dunkirk, June 1940

We helped rescue the British Army,
my dad, the *Mayflower* and me.

We were one of those little ships
in a flotilla that put to sea.

We took on-board the soldiers
left stranded on the beaches of France.

When destroyers couldn't reach them
we were able to advance.

Beneath a hail of bullets
that rained down on the sea,

we helped rescue the British Army,
my dad, the *Mayflower* and me.

Brian Moses

*During the Battle of Dunkirk,
hundreds of thousands of Allied
soldiers were trapped between
the German Army and the sea
in Dunkirk, France. To help
evacuate the soldiers, hundreds of
small fishing vessels and lifeboats
were called into action alongside
the British Navy, rescuing over
300,000 troops.*

Safe

'We'll be safe,' I heard Dad say,
'from all but a direct hit.'

Safe, I thought, how can we
be safe?
Already we're buried
under two feet of earth,
Dad's cabbages growing on top.

Already it feels
as if we're in our tomb,
in this shelter we sleep in
each night.

Hearing the crump
of explosions,
like giant's footsteps
shaking the ground
and edging closer.

I have a life worth living
and I will survive,
I tell myself.

But how on earth did I think
that war might be fun,
tucked beneath the ground
like rabbits in a burrow?

'If a bomb's got our name on it . . .'
I heard Mum say to Dad,
and although she never
finished the sentence,
I knew what she meant.

But was it right, I wondered,
to hope that a bomb
had someone else's name
on it?

Brian Moses

Night after Night after Night

I remember the wailing sirens, the hurried waking,
the stumbling down the street with blankets
in our arms and pushing our way into the shelter.
I remember the dog howling from the house
when we weren't allowed to take her with us.
I remember the interrupted nights,
my bedroom, the shelter, then back in my bed again.
I remember the anger of the guns as they desperately
    tried
to turn back the bombers or throw them off target.
I remember the whistle and whine of the bombs that
    fell,
the fear that the nearest explosion could have been
    our house.
I remember the all-clear, the peering from the doorway
to see if the street had suffered, if the houses still stood.
I remember the men raking through the wreckage,
the relief that our house had its doors and
    windows intact.
I remember the dust and the smoke from the
    fires that still burned.
I remember thinking, does it even the score,
    if we do the same
to German cities? Will it help *us* win this war?

Brian Moses

During the Blitz in 1940, London was bombed for fifty-seven nights in a row.
Over a million homes were damaged or destroyed and more than 40,000
Londoners died.

A Message to Adolf

When photographs were published of Londoners,
they were never looking gloomy or depressed,
never looking fed up or exhausted
or wearied by the nightly lack of rest.

The mood was always one of optimism,
bombed out we may be but we're not down.
We'll do anything to keep our spirits up,
show everyone a smile and not a frown.

We can take it, so Hitler do your worst,
you're mistaken if you think that you can win.
All that you can do will never be enough:
the British people will never give in.

Brian Moses

*Newspapers were discouraged from showing too many pictures of bomb
damage or people looking unhappy, injured or depressed.*

Airmen

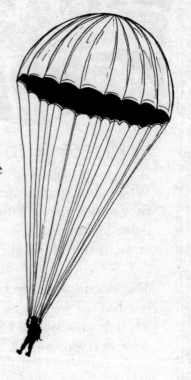

As the sun set
We watched the plane
Spiral out of control
Heard the clump
As it hit the ground
Beyond the wood

Saw the thin plume of smoke
Grey, laced with pink
Rising above the crash
Like a question mark
Then we saw the parachute
Caught in the sun
Like a drifting star
And that night in bed
I listened to the whistles
As they searched the wood
For that German airman

I imagined him being frightened
Far from home
And I pulled my eiderdown
Around me
And thought of Dad
And offered up a prayer
For lonely airmen
Everywhere

Roger Stevens

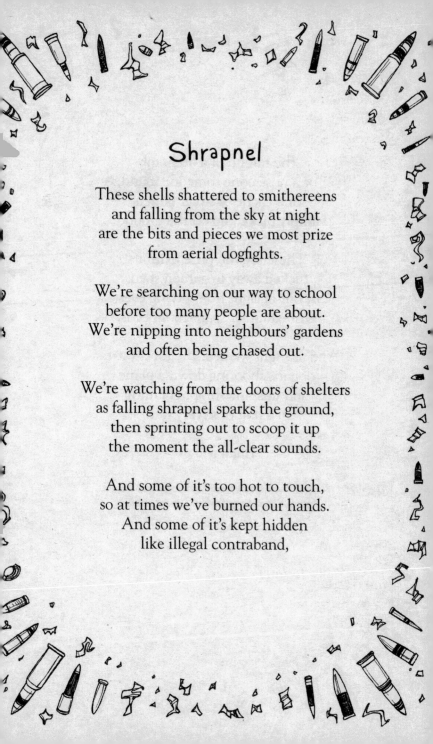

Shrapnel

These shells shattered to smithereens
and falling from the sky at night
are the bits and pieces we most prize
from aerial dogfights.

We're searching on our way to school
before too many people are about.
We're nipping into neighbours' gardens
and often being chased out.

We're watching from the doors of shelters
as falling shrapnel sparks the ground,
then sprinting out to scoop it up
the moment the all-clear sounds.

And some of it's too hot to touch,
so at times we've burned our hands.
And some of it's kept hidden
like illegal contraband,

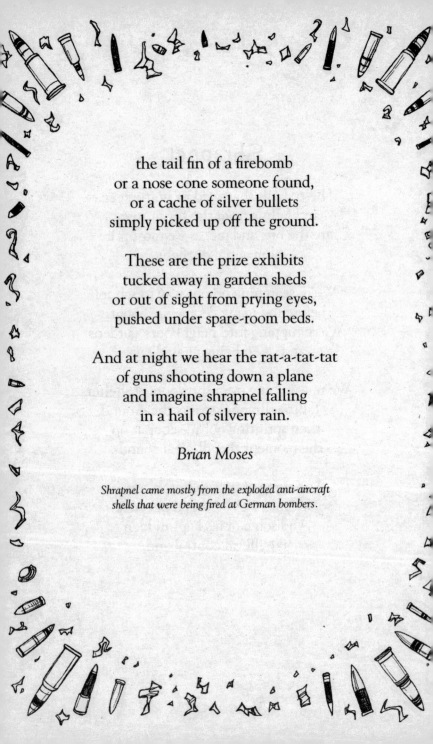

the tail fin of a firebomb
or a nose cone someone found,
or a cache of silver bullets
simply picked up off the ground.

These are the prize exhibits
tucked away in garden sheds
or out of sight from prying eyes,
pushed under spare-room beds.

And at night we hear the rat-a-tat-tat
of guns shooting down a plane
and imagine shrapnel falling
in a hail of silvery rain.

Brian Moses

*Shrapnel came mostly from the exploded anti-aircraft
shells that were being fired at German bombers.*

Eating Carrots

It's why we need to eat carrots,
Mum says,
so we can see in the blackout.

But I remember reading
in the *Boys' Book of Knowledge*
how it would take a lifetime
of eating carrots,
and not just a few, but thousands,
to make a real difference.

Mum doesn't listen,
she won't see sense.
She cooks carrot tart, carrot flan,
carrot mash, carrot jam,
carrot cake, carrot surprise (it never is!),
carrot chutney, carrot rissoles,
carrot pie, carrot sausages,
carrot jelly, carrot omelette,
carrot scones, carrot loaf,
carrot crumble, carrot sponge
and carrot marmalade.

Then she tells us
we'll notice a difference soon.

But the only time I can see
in the dark
is under the glow from
a friendly moon,
and it's still as black as it always was
in my blacked out room.

Brian Moses

*During the Second World War, the British government
spread propaganda saying that eating carrots would
help you to see in the dark. This was to cover up the
development of radar technology, which allowed British
pilots to pinpoint the location on enemy planes in the dark.*

Learner Drivers

A trail of smashed milk bottles
The pavement's milky wet
Billy's football squashed and burst
Billy's quite upset

Mrs Jones's geraniums
Fit for the compost heap
Mum's vase bounced off the sideboard
You should have seen it leap

And Grandad's bicycle's been crushed
He's in a proper fix
And the wall where Grandad leaned his bike
Is now a pile of bricks

Three lamp posts bent like coat hangers
Our cat has run away
You have to learn to drive a tank
And the lessons were today

Roger Stevens

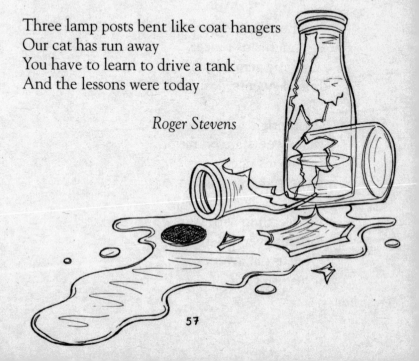

Sweets

The government says
I can only have
two ounces of **sweets**
a week.

That's far too few
so all day through
I constantly dream
of **sweets**.

Forget 'Doctor Carrot'
and 'Potato Pete'.
What will do me good
is a bag of **sweets**.

I smile charmingly
at Americans I meet,
'Got any gum, chum?'
I need **sweets**.

It isn't right
that **sweets** are on ration.
It's sugar I need,
sweets are my passion.

I'm pleading with you
for kids everywhere.
Give us our **sweets**,
it just isn't fair.

I know that in war
we must smile and make do,
but a few extra toffees
or another chew

wouldn't hurt the war effort,
surely not,
and for all us kids
it would mean a lot!

But the government says
our ration is enough;
for MPs maybe
but for kids, it's tough.

Brian Moses

*Two ounces is equal to fifty-seven grams,
about the same weight as eight two-pence pieces.*

Women's Work

Building bridges
Making fences
Searchlight, ack-ack
Air defences
Air-raid wardens
Taking chances
Driving cars
And ambulances
Fixing cars
Changing tyres
Electricians
Changing wires
Fire brigade
To put out fires
Eighty thousand
On the farms
In factories
Making arms
Making uniforms
And boots
Carefully packing
Parachutes

Of all the jobs
That men back then
Thought only men could do
Not unsurprisingly
It turned out, women
Could do them too.

Roger Stevens

*Before the Second World War, women were expected
to be housewives, secretaries, nurses or shop assistants.
But when men were called upon to fight, women were
called upon to fill their jobs, many of which were
previously thought to be unsuitable for women.*

Salvage

They told us our country needed metal
from a large park railing to a tiny tin kettle,
that everything had its place in a chain
and when melted down might be used in a plane.

So we made our collections, buckets and cans,
old metal baths, wheels from go-carts and prams,
my tin soldiers, the pot for our stew,
our kettle, a spade and an old horseshoe.

And it pleased us to think that all those things
might one day be part of a Spitfire's wings,
and that we would wonder which bit of metal
might previously have been our tin kettle.

Brian Moses

My Father's War

*My father was a male nurse in the Royal Army Medical Corps
in the Second World War*

My father fought his desert war,
picked up and patched up casualties.
It didn't matter what side they were on,
a wounded man was a wounded man,
Tunisia through to Italy.

In makeshift tents he spent his nights
with dying men, fighting his war on war,
winning back hope for the ones who felt
they'd lost everything, who glimpsed
in the owl-faced nurse a confessor, a friend.

Death dresses soldiers alike
in uniforms of ashen grey and white.
Those who died were quickly covered,
small mounds, a hymn, a prayer,
souls took wing to London or Berlin.

My father, in the grainy sepia snaps,
El Alamein through to Cassino,
then back by road across Europe,
glimpses of war-damaged towns
through gaps in a lorry's canvas flaps.

Over the years he blocked the horror,
kept it to himself and shared instead
the friendship, the sightseeing,
his Christmas lunch in Austria,
his blessing from the Pope.

And I regret all those times I closed
my ears – should have realized instead
how he never gloried in what he'd done,
just retold his war; tried to understand
what would never be understood.

Brian Moses

The Women's Land Army

We could do with thousands more like you
Is what the poster said
We need crops to feed the troops
And wheat to make the bread
The men are all off fighting
What are you waiting for?
Join the Women's Land Army
And help us win the war

I joined in nineteen thirty-nine
For thirty bob a week
Growing peas and beans and carrots
Cabbages and leeks
I could wrestle a reluctant sheep
When shearing time was nigh
Milk a cow, collect the eggs
Muck out the horses and the sty

I could strip a tractor engine
From carburettor to the coil
I could park it on a sixpence
Change the spark plugs and the oil
Women working on the land
Could show the men a thing or two
I could shoot a rat from twenty yards
I was called 'Quick Draw McGrew'

We dug the land and sowed and hoed
And harvested the grain
For fifty hours a week we worked
In cold and frost and rain
And when the sun was shining
What fun it was to be
Helping the war effort
In the Women's Land Army

Roger Stevens

*Thirty bob was slang for thirty shillings (£1.50 in today's
money). In the past people earned less, but things also
cost less. Today this would be the equivalent of earning
£80 a week.*

Wartime Food

Could you eat a wartime diet?
Would you enjoy the food they ate?
Dried eggs instead of fresh ones,
whale meat instead of steak?

Tinned snoek with nettle purée,
or a nasty potato-peel pie.
Coffee from acorns or parsnips
when there wasn't any to buy.

The sea could offer limpets,
like gum without the taste,
chewing them would leave your mouth
glued up like sticky paste.

Carrageen moss, a sort of seaweed,
mixed with milk could make blancmange,
and spider crabs when cooked
would certainly make you cringe.

Shredded sprouts, beetroot sandwiches,
a glass of raw swede juice,
Potatoes with pig's liver baked in a pie
and labelled 'Poor Man's Goose'.

Then finish with a cup of bramble tea
and be grateful you still survive.
Food may have been unpalatable
but at least it kept you alive.

Brian Moses

*Snoek – a tinned variety of a fish from South Africa called
barracouta*

*Foods such as carrageen moss and limpets were eaten in the
Channel Islands towards the end of the German occupation,
when there were extreme shortages of food.*

The Animal Victoria Cross

And to Simon
Who served
On HMS *Amethyst*
Who survived cannon shell
Raised morale
And despite injury
Dealt very well
With an infestation of rats
We award
The Dickin Medal
For bravery
For being
An exceptionally cat-like
Cat.

Roger Stevens

*The Dickin Medal for animal bravery
was the animal equivalent of the
Victoria Cross. It was awarded to
thirty-two pigeons, eighteen dogs, three
horses and one cat.*

Pigeon

Percy is our last pigeon
And I often come up to the pigeon loft
For a chat

Now Dad's gone
Mum says
We'll not be having
Any more pigeons
When Percy finally leaves us

I tell our pigeon about Mary of Exeter
A pigeon who fought in the war
Well, not exactly fought

Mary brought secret messages home from France
She was shot down once, but still made it back
And once she was four days late
After an attack by a falcon
And once she was hit by shrapnel
But still got back in one piece
She had twenty-two stitches
And won the Dickin Medal

I wonder if Percy is jealous
Or is he pleased he missed it all?
Maybe I'm the jealous one

Jealous that Mary of Exeter
Made it back from the war
But Dad didn't

Roger Stevens

*After Mary's war service her owner made her a
leather collar to support her injured neck and head.
She lived until 1950 and was buried with full
military honours.*

Doodlebug

Look, there it is
A tiny speck in the sky, growing larger
Like some weird black beetle on the wing
Flying in a dead straight line

Listen, now you hear it
A drone
Like a disturbed wasp's nest
And growing louder
As it passes over

Sigh, with relief
Because if the drone stops
You run like hell
And hope you're you fast enough
To escape the doodlebug's
Deadly sting

Roger Stevens

Doodlebugs, also known as V-1 flying bombs, were an early kind of jet-propelled bomb. Their engines made a buzzing noise like a large insect. When the noise stopped, it meant the bomb was about to explode.

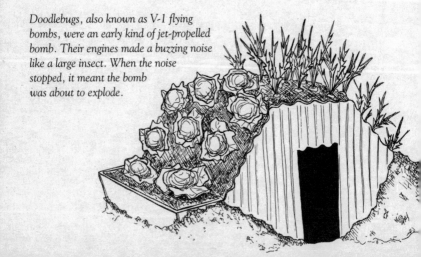

Miss Leaky Mouth

Miss Leaky Mouth will blab
so be careful what you say.
Don't try to confide in her,
don't give anything away.

She just can't keep her mouth shut,
she can't control her tongue.
Let her in on a secret
and she'll tell everyone.

In wartime walls have ears,
it's something we recognize.
That ordinary guy she's talking to
might well be in disguise.

Spies will be almost anywhere
and listen to anything.
Miss Leaky Mouth's a canary,
she'll open her mouth and sing.

Her lips are loose so never say
what you wouldn't want repeated.
Careless talk costs lives (it's true)
and we could be defeated.

Brian Moses

*Miss Leaky Mouth was a cartoon character in the Second
World War, warning everyone about the danger of giving
information to strangers, in case they turned out to be enemy spies.*

A Pocketful of Soil

We empty it into the garden
When the guards' backs are turned
We are digging a tunnel with cutlery

A pocketful of soil
A pocketful of soil
A pocketful of soil at a time

We are already six feet under the library
Library? A few dozen tattered paperbacks
Sent by the Red Cross

A pocketful of soil
A pocketful of soil
A pocketful of soil at a time

Time is our friend
A football match, a game of chess
We measure it in pockets full of soil

A pocketful of soil
A pocketful of soil
A pocketful of soil at a time

Three hundred yards to go
To get beyond the wire, the searchlights
The gun turrets, to get to freedom

A pocketful of soil
A pocketful of soil
A pocketful of soil at a time

Roger Stevens

*Prisoners of War (also known as PoWs) were
people who had been captured by enemy forces.
They were kept in prison camps and sometimes
they tried to escape by digging tunnels.*

Carrots

From a photograph of a boy in Warsaw, Poland,
stealing carrots for his family

Just a boy
on a Warsaw street,
he shook his shirt
and the carrots spilled out.

And the soldiers who grasped his shoulders,
who had enough food on their tables,
looked down at the carrots
tumbling from his sleeves,
from the pockets of his jacket,
from the waistband of his trousers.

And they photographed him,
the lad from the ghetto,
stealing carrots
so his family might eat.

And I could see,
in the twisted faces of the soldiers,
that he was about to receive
some terrible punishment.

And I thought about me,
when I was his age.
Would I have done
what he did?
Fought for food,
risked everything
for just carrots?

Brian Moses

*During the Second World War, many Jewish
families in Poland, Germany and Austria were
imprisoned in overcrowded ghettos before being
moved to concentration camps. There was little
food and so families would often have to beg or
steal to survive.*

Subterfuge

Fooled you!
We fooled you!
Those tanks weren't real
They were made of wood
We fooled you, yes
We fooled you good.

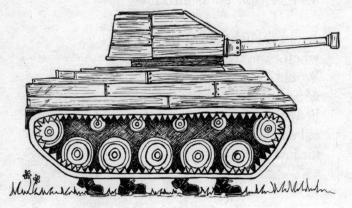

And the real tanks
Were in disguise
Didn't you know
Or realize
That the desert sun
Can play tricks
With your eyes?

Roger Stevens

*During the Second World War, the military constructed
whole units of fake tanks. Real tanks were also disguised
using fabric to look like normal road vehicles.*

VE Day

It was . . .
Lancaster bombers dropping red and green flares,
the peeling of bells, the whistle of tugs on the Thames.
It was . . .
Sailors climbing lamp posts, swinging by one arm,
policemen losing their helmets.
It was . . .
Bonfires lit, fireworks fizzling, dustbin lids clanging,
washing lines strung with red, white and blue clothes.
It was . . .
Paddling in the fountains in Trafalgar Square,
men's faces covered in lipstick kisses.
It was. . .
Grandad tearfully singing 'The White Cliffs of Dover'
and being pushed home from the celebrations
in a wheelbarrow.

Brian Moses

VE Day, which stands for Victory in Europe Day, was a public holiday held in
Europe on the 8 May 1945 to celebrate the unconditional surrender of the
German forces.

Shadows

Children playing in the street
In Hiroshima or Nagasaki
A mother's call
A clear blue sky
A bomb
(Just one – that's all)
Like a giant camera flash
And children's shadows
Burned upon a wall

Roger Stevens

*In August 1945 the Americans dropped two atomic bombs
on Japan, ending the Second World War. This is the only
time that nuclear weapons have ever been used in warfare.*

What Are We Fighting For?

'I object to violence because when it appears to do good, the good is only temporary; the evil it does is permanent'

Mahatma Gandhi

The War Factor

In comics, in the fifties, the Japanese would yell,
  'Banzai!'
And they'd blow the US trucks out of the way
But the Yanks are on a mission, they find the
  enemy's munitions
And KA-BOOM! Their army's now in disarray

In films, like *Spartacus*, *Ben-Hur* or *Gladiator*
We watch with glee the Romans' power play
Meanwhile Roman legions crush all the
  neighbouring regions
And woe betide the slaves who disobey

In old films we watch the British in India or Africa
Where they rule the democratic British way
And the US bomb the Viet Cong and decimate the
    jungle
As Hollywood performs its cabaret

And my computer game's amazing, it's as though
    I'm really there
My army's getting stronger every day
You can hear the shrapnel flying and the crying of
    the dying
Fact or fiction? Sometimes it's hard to say

In comics, films and books, it seems we need an
    enemy to fight
War becomes a game that we can play
It seems war's an entertainment, an amusement,
    an escape
When reality starts getting in the way

Roger Stevens

Don't You Know
There's a War on?

My mother didn't know there was a war on.
She hung out the washing on the line
as I crouched among the cabbages
and gave covering fire.

My father didn't know there was a war on.
He called out, 'Hello,' as he came in from work
and I broke cover, shouted back,
ignoring the cracking of bullets.

The dog didn't know there was a war on.
He carried on sniffing in no-man's-land
then lifted a leg on the sign I'd painted
to warn of danger from mines.

The neighbours didn't know there was a war on.
They hung over the fence and complained
that one of my missiles went AWOL
and drove its way through their dahlias.

After that I packed in the war,
ran up a white flag and agreed to end
hostilities for the day. I pulled out my troops
from the flower-bed, brought the dead back
to life, then boxed them and went indoors.

There wasn't much for tea and when
I complained, Mum snapped, 'I thought you said
there's a war on, so how am I supposed
to bring supplies through a battle zone?'

Later I watched *The News* on TV.
It seemed there was a war on everywhere.
Perhaps I'll declare an outbreak of peace tomorrow.

Brian Moses

AWOL – absent without leave, gone missing

Missiles in Cuba

I was twelve years old
when Kennedy muscled up to Khrushchev over
    missiles in Cuba,
when Cold War bluff and counter-bluff took the world
    to the brink.
I learned a new word:
Armageddon.
'It could happen here,'
the papers proclaimed,
'It could happen now.'
I questioned my parents constantly, were we all about
    to die?
My father, grim-faced,
spoke only of the last lot,
of how they survived.
But the world had rolled on since then, more fuses,
    more firepower.
My eyes pleaded with him,
say it will be OK.
But he was frightened too,
I could tell.

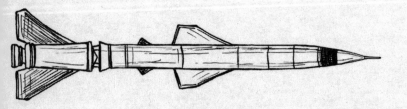

We tiptoed about the house,
it didn't seem right to play Elvis songs,
no 'Good Luck Charm' would stop this war,
I knew the score on that one.
And why should I worry about tests at school, we
    could all be blown to pieces
come the weekend.
My father said it was prayer that was needed,
but prayer wasn't doing any good.
And I remember that last-chance Sunday, all of us
    praying in church,
praying so hard it hurt,
then coming home to find
they'd backed away, stepped down from the abyss.

Out in the garden
I stood beneath the stars, breathed in,
breathed deep,
breathed a future.

Brian Moses

*In 1962 the Russians started building nuclear-missile sites on Cuba, a
communist island only ninety miles away from America. This was because
the Americans had placed nuclear missiles in Turkey aimed at Moscow.
People were scared it might be the start of a nuclear war.*

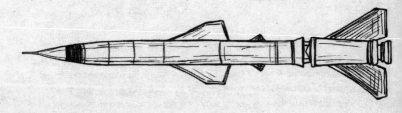

Vietnam Veterans' Memorial

Some people in the USA
Said better dead than red
And they thought that communists
Were underneath their beds

Now in Constitution Gardens
In a park in Washington
There's a memorial for veterans
Who died in Vietnam

Nearly sixty thousand soldiers
And every soldier's name
Better dead than red?
Ask the ghosts of those dead soldiers
If they still feel the same

Roger Stevens

*The colour red is associated with communism and can be found on
many flags of communist countries such as the Soviet Union and China.
Communism is both a type of government and an economic system (a
way of creating and sharing wealth) in which everyone is supposed to
share the wealth they create so no one has more or less than anyone else.*

Sniper

Mum gives Tarik a hug
Don't cross the square
It may be further via the church
But it's safe. You're not in open view.

And tell him, Belma sends her love
That might be worth an extra loaf or two
I know he has the flour still
And while you are there
Ask him, What news of Ivan?

Mum gives Tarik another hug
And whispers a short prayer
Go now, she says
And do not cross the square

Roger Stevens

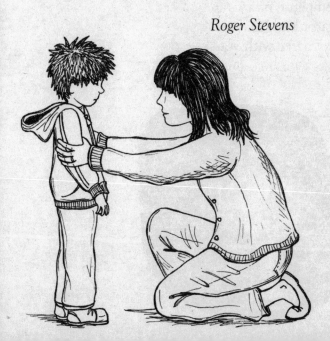

Hide-and-Seek

You are hiding
In a confined space
It's cramped, uncomfortable
But no one is counting to a hundred
Coming! Ready or not!
Because it's not a game.
You may have to stay there
Silent and still
For an hour
Or a week
Or a year
And you are probably wondering
What you did wrong?
It's because you were born a Christian,
Or maybe a Muslim, or maybe a Jew
And an emperor, or a king
Or a dictator has decided
They don't agree with you

Roger Stevens

The War on Terror

To kill
Innocent
Men
And women and children
To tape a bomb
To your body
And walk into
A busy market
To fly
An aeroplane
Into a skyscraper
How strong
Your belief must be

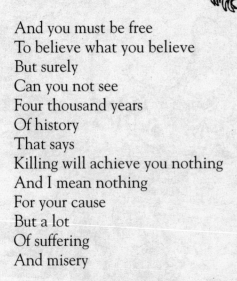

And you must be free
To believe what you believe
But surely
Can you not see
Four thousand years
Of history
That says
Killing will achieve you nothing
And I mean nothing
For your cause
But a lot
Of suffering
And misery

Roger Stevens

Deadly Duo

Stealth bomber
You are like an owl
A ghostly shape
Swooping on your prey

Owl
You are a stealth bomber
The shrew looks up
Too late

Roger Stevens

Escalation

Billy took my apple
So I kicked Billy in the shins.

Billy's mate pushed me over
On the playground
And I dropped my lunch box

So my mate Dave
Punched Billy's mate
On the nose

Then all Billy's friends joined in
And so did mine
And everyone was fighting

And Jess was shouting
And screaming for me
And Tess told her to 'Shut up!'

And soon the girls were all at it too
And the dinner ladies came to sort it out
But Mrs Pickings said it was my fault

And Miss Brodie told her that she saw it all
And it wasn't and they started arguing
And Mrs Pickings hit her with her handbag

And the teachers had to come and sort it out
And it took a while
Because they were all arguing too

Luckily Mr Walton heard the rumpus
Came out of his office
And blew his whistle

And it all got sorted in the end
And me and Billy shook hands and said sorry
And he whispered to me

After school . . .
You're dead!

Roger Stevens

The Shouting Side

There's a war being waged
in our family,
Mum versus Dad,
in the middle there's me
and it's hard to decide
whose side I'm on
when they're both
on the shouting side.

Dad shouts at Mum,
Mum screams at Dad,
then they start on me
and it makes me mad,
I don't want to decide
whose side I'm on
when they're both
on the shouting side.

Can't they see,
can't they be quiet?
Why do they yell
like they're starting a riot?
They're acting this out
on a tiny stage,
there's no need to shout
or fly into a rage.

There's no need to take out
their feelings on me,
I'm trying to listen,
can't they see?
I'm standing here
with my ears wide open,
somebody please
be quietly spoken.

There's a war being waged
in our family,
Mum versus Dad,
in the middle there's me
and it's hard to decide
whose side I'm on
when they're both
on the shouting side.

Brian Moses

What Causes War?

Lust for power
Lust for land
How much soil
Does one man need?

Lust for gold
Lust for oil
There's no excuse
In one word – 'greed'

And religion too
Must share the blame
The sacred words
Ignored

Or changed to suit
The moneymakers
Building guns
And swords

As troubles breed
And wars increase
We need to know
What causes peace?

Roger Stevens

Spoils of War

Imagine, after humans have left the planet
And the new owners of Earth
Are digging about for signs of our past

There will probably be a TV programme
Intergalactic Time Team
Beamed across the universe

Aliens, delicately sifting soil
Looking for ancient artefacts
Trying to discover what our race was like

Excitement as the first items are found
An ancient sword, bullets, a rusted flamethrower
An unexploded mine

Roger Stevens

What Are We Fighting For?

What are we fighting for?
>We have to do or die.

What are we fighting for?
>We can't turn a blind eye.

What are we fighting for?
>To sleep safely in bed.

What are we fighting for?
>To keep away fear and dread.

What are we fighting for?
>To keep our children free.

What are we fighting for?
>To choose our own destiny.

What are we fighting for?
>Because there's nowhere to hide.

What are we fighting for?
>Because so many have died.

What are we fighting for?
>To challenge oppression.

What are we fighting for?
>To combat aggression.

What are we fighting for?
>To win us the war.

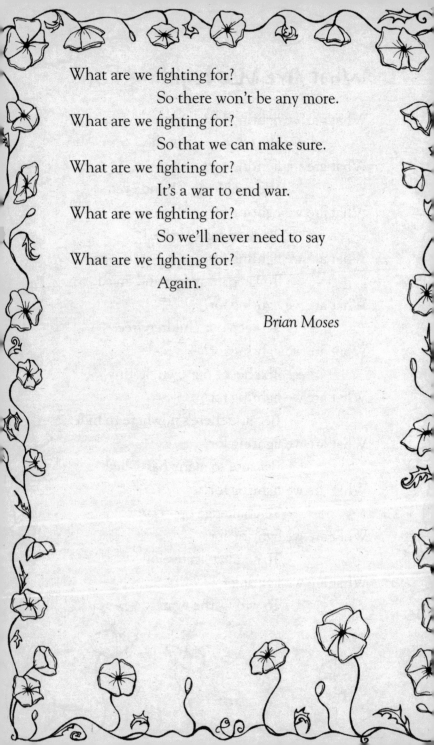

What are we fighting for?
        So there won't be any more.
What are we fighting for?
        So that we can make sure.
What are we fighting for?
        It's a war to end war.
What are we fighting for?
        So we'll never need to say
What are we fighting for?
        Again.

Brian Moses

Index of First Lines